Olga Moves House

OTHER OLGA DA POLGA STORIES

Olga Moves House

Michael Bond
Illustrated by Hans Helweg

OXFORD
UNIVERSITY PRESS

OXFORD

UNIVERSITY PRESS

Great Clarendon Street, Oxford OX2 6DP

Oxford University Press is a department of the University of Oxford.
It furthers the University's objective of excellence in research, scholarship,
and education by publishing worldwide in

Oxford   New York

Auckland   Cape Town   Dar es Salaam   Hong Kong   Karachi
Kuala Lumpur   Madrid   Melbourne   Mexico City   Nairobi
New Delhi   Shanghai   Taipei   Toronto

With offices in

Argentina   Austria   Brazil   Chile   Czech Republic   France   Greece
Guatemala   Hungary   Italy   Japan   Poland   Portugal   Singapore
South Korea   Switzerland   Thailand   Turkey   Ukraine   Vietnam

Oxford is a registered trademark of Oxford University Press
in the UK and in certain other countries

First published 2001
First published in this edition 2007

5

British Library Cataloguing in Publication Data available

ISBN 978-0-19-275491-2

Designed and typeset by Mike Brain Graphic Design Limited, Oxford
Printed in Great Britain by Clays Ltd, Elcograf S.p.A.

CONTENTS

For Peter Gurney

1
Olga Does It Herself

No one in the Sawdust family could remember exactly when it happened, but happen it did. One moment Olga was living in her hutch in the garden, the next moment she had moved into their house. Once there, she made herself very much at home in a corner of the dining-room; as large as life 'thank you very much', and often—especially when it was getting near meal times—twice as noisy.

Olga could have told them how it came about. But then, being a guinea-pig, she had more reason to remember it than most. When your life suddenly changes the way hers had done you don't forget it in a hurry. She could still picture the moment very clearly.

It happened one evening when the Sawdust family went out, leaving her on her own, and as was so often the case when she was left on her own, she took to eating her hay and wondering about things in general. Olga was very fond of hay. She always found eating it not only helped pass the time, it also gave her lots of ideas.

Afterwards, and again, as often happened when the sun went down and it got cold, she wished she hadn't. That night, for whatever reason, they were late getting back. In fact, they were so late she had almost given up hope of ever seeing them again. And to make matters worse, she had eaten all her bedding.

When they did appear they made a great fuss of her, bringing her indoors so that her bedroom could be made ready for the night—

her food and water bowls 'topped up', and her supply of bedding replenished.

Except most of those things never happened.

Having been passed around from hand to hand, first to Karen Sawdust, then Mr Sawdust, and finally to Mrs Sawdust, it was decided that before anything else, Olga needed warming up.

Mrs Sawdust found what she called 'a suitable cardboard box', which she laid on its side near a radiator in a corner of the dining-room, leaving one of the flaps open so that it not only acted as a front door step, but also let in the heat. Then she spread a thick layer of newspaper on the floor in front of the box in case 'certain of us' had an accident during the night with their water bowl.

After that, Mr Sawdust covered the bottom of the box with a double layer of wood chippings. 'Especially formulated for the comfort and well-being of guinea-pigs,' he announced, reading from the outside of the packet. 'You can't say fairer than that.'

At the time Olga could hardly believe her

good fortune, for suddenly, hey presto, there she was, as snug as a bug in a rug! It was just like having a tiny house within a house, and it even had its own front garden.

She decided to make the most of it, for she fully expected to be put back in her outside hutch the very next day, but somehow that never happened.

Really, it was all most satisfactory.

'I don't suppose there are many guinea-pigs "living in" as part of the family,' she was fond of saying to anyone who happened to be passing and had time to listen. 'Especially not with all mod. cons.'

Olga had no idea what 'mod. cons.' were, but

she knew they were nice things to have because one day, soon after the change-over had taken place, she overheard Mrs Sawdust talking to a man who had come to read the gas meter.

'It's all right for some,' he said, looking at Olga's house. 'You mark my words. She'll be wanting her meter read next!'

In the end it was Mr Sawdust who came up with the answer. 'If you remember, it was when we had that sudden cold snap,' he said. 'We were late back from the cinema, so we brought Olga indoors to get warm . . .'

'And you didn't want to clean out her hutch before she went to bed,' said Mrs Sawdust.

'I like that!' replied Mr Sawdust. 'It was snowing hard and nobody else was exactly rushing for the dustpan and brush. Anyway, whatever the reason, it's too late to change now.'

'It's hard to picture it being any other way,' said Karen Sawdust.

'It wouldn't be the same at all,' agreed Mrs Sawdust. 'I don't know why we didn't do it at the very beginning.'

Olga felt relieved as she listened in to the conversation. She certainly didn't want to change her present arrangements. With both Graham, the tortoise, and Fangio, the hedgehog, fast asleep for the winter, there was no one much to talk to during the day and she went back to munching her oats.

But her peace was short lived, for as soon as the meal was over Karen Sawdust picked her up so that she could sit on her lap and watch television.

'Wheeeeee.' Olga gave a squeak of excitement. That was something else she hadn't been able to do in her hutch—watch television. If she were in charge of things she would certainly make sure all guinea-pigs had television. It was a way of seeing the world without ever having to move.

She wondered if it might be a football programme. That was one of her favourites. Although why people had to keep running all over the grass instead of sitting down to eat it she couldn't imagine. Given a choice, she much

preferred watching snooker because there wasn't so much shouting.

'Guinea-pigs used to be very good at playing snooker,' she said one day to Noel, the cat, when she was feeling in a boastful mood and wanted to put him in his place. 'Until we invented it nobody had ever thought of putting grass on tables before.'

'Grass!' said Noel scornfully. 'It isn't grass, it's cloth. I heard Mr Sawdust talking about it. Anyway, he said you're supposed to keep one foot on the ground when you play. Guinea-pigs couldn't keep one leg on the ground, let alone a foot.'

Noel looked on Olga's presence as an invasion of his territory and he lost no opportunity to air his superior knowledge whenever he could.

'When we invented snooker,' said Olga, not to be outdone, 'it used to be played on grass and the tables were very low. The Sawdust people only put legs on them when they saw what a good game it was and started playing it themselves.'

But as things turned out the programme she watched that evening was neither football nor snooker. It was called Do-it-Yourself and although she didn't see so much as a single blade of grass the whole time it was on, Olga had to admit she found it very interesting.

It was all about a lady who was decorating her room. First she painted all the walls different colours. Then she put new curtains up. Finally, to show how easy it was, she did the whole thing all over again, only this time very, very quickly.

'I think Olga enjoyed that,' said Karen Sawdust as she put her back down on the floor. 'She didn't blink once the whole time it was on.'

But Olga was hardly listening. Her mind was in a whirl. Having retired to her box, she lay down in the hay and looked around. Until that moment she had been very happy with her surroundings, but she had to admit that compared to the room she had just seen it was really very dull. Even the Sawdust family's room, with its light green walls—*sponge effect* Mrs Sawdust called it—was brighter than hers. It was one of the many things she enjoyed most about living with them, for it was like being in an open field without having your whiskers ruffled all the time by the wind.

All the same, she couldn't get the room she had seen on television out of her mind.

If only I could do it *my*self, she thought. I expect I would soon have the nicest room in the nicest house in the whole, wide world.

Later that night, when everyone had gone to bed, Olga set to work. Luckily there was a full moon outside and the light shining through the windows was just enough for her to see what she was doing.

Taking hold of a piece of carrot, still wet from where she had been chewing it, she rubbed the end against the side of her cardboard box. It made a very satisfactory mark.

Next, she tried doing the same thing with some beetroot, and that was better still. Even in the half-light she could see the difference. In fact, she was so pleased with her handiwork she ate the rest of it by mistake and had to go back to using the carrot.

Olga had no doubt in her mind that the Sawdust family would be very surprised when they came down in the morning and discovered what she had done.

It was then, when she leaned back to take another look, that the worst happened.

She let out a loud 'Wheeeeeeeeeeeeeeeeee!' as she stepped into her water bowl. The water went everywhere and she jumped so high in the air she landed in the middle of her bowl of seeds. That went all over the place too. The mixture of water and seeds went over the sawdust and the wood chippings, over the newspaper, and, worst of all, over her hay.

The shrieks and the bangs and crashes and the sound of breaking crockery echoed round

the house and brought the Sawdust family running.

'Olga! What have you been up to?' cried Karen Sawdust. 'I've never seen such a mess!'

'Mess!' squeaked Olga. 'Mess! Wheeeee-eeee! It's *Do-it-Myself*!'

'I tell you something,' said Mrs Sawdust, when she saw what had been going on. 'It's given me an idea.'

After she'd had a good wipe down, Olga was given another box to dry out in, and the very next morning it was Mrs Sawdust's turn to set to work.

Olga was put into another room and soon afterwards she noticed a strange smell, the like of which she hadn't come across before. It wasn't a very nice smell, and she was glad when Mrs Sawdust cut an onion in half and made it disappear.

Then, at long last, came the big moment.

Olga could hardly believe her eyes, and this time her 'Wheeeeeeeeeee!' was one of joy.

While she had been in the other room the outside of her new home had been painted so that it matched the walls of the Sawdust family's living room. It even blended in with the carpet, so that it was hard to tell where one ended and the other began.

Inside, if she looked really hard, she could still see the marks she had made with the carrot and the beetroot on the wall of her bedroom.

From that moment on there really was no going back. Olga decided it wasn't so much *Do-it-Myself* as *Doing-it-Ourselves*. And that, to her mind, was the nicest thing of all, because now she really did feel part of the family.

2

The Story of Olga's Nose

Life in the Sawdust household normally followed a strict routine, especially in the mornings. Mrs Sawdust was always first down and she started work straight away, preparing breakfast for the rest of the family.

It suited Olga very well. Being a creature of habit, she liked everything to be in its proper place and for things to happen at the same time every day, otherwise you didn't know where you were, and she soon began to recognize certain sounds.

Even though Mrs Sawdust did her best to

make as little noise as possible, taking care not to rattle the cutlery or clink the china, the slightest sound—like the opening of the refrigerator door, was enough to make Olga prick up her ears. She knew very well that if she squeaked loud enough and long enough, she would be given a dandelion leaf or some other delicacy to keep her quiet until the rest of the family were ready to eat.

'I always wake at the first creak,' she explained to Noel, the cat, when he complained about it. 'We guinea-pigs have good ear-sight.'

'Too good, if you ask me,' said Noel. 'Anyway, how do you know it's the first creak?' To which she had no answer.

Then one day she noticed a change had come over the normal pattern of things. Gone were the clinks and clanks she had come to expect, and what was even worse, her squeaks had no effect at all.

Suddenly her world had gone topsy turvy, and she no longer knew where she was or what was going to happen next.

In fact, it was because a stool had been left in the middle of the kitchen that Olga ran into it and banged her nose on one of the legs, but since that in turn led to her telling one of her best ever stories she couldn't really grumble.

She had got used to watching Mrs Sawdust getting breakfast, and the first thing she noticed was the smell. It wasn't there any more.

Instead, Mrs Sawdust spent a lot of time counting things she called 'calories', whatever they were, and try as she might Olga was unable to see any. However, the whole family appeared to have been eating far too many and it wasn't doing them any good.

Listening to the others talking, she discovered they were on something called a diet, which meant eating less of everything. Olga didn't like the sound of it at all.

Mr Sawdust started doing something called 'weighing himself on the bathroom scales' and one day he came downstairs looking very gloomy indeed. Soon after that he took to going out early in the morning. He was dressed in the sort of clothes he normally only wore on very hot summer days when he was doing the gardening; the thinnest of tops, very short trousers, and white shoes which made him bounce up and down when he walked.

But the most worrying thing of all was that several times Olga heard her own name being mentioned.

'I've said it before,' remarked Mr Sawdust, when he arrived home one morning mopping his brow and heard her squeaking for breakfast, 'and I'll say it again. It wouldn't do Olga any harm if she lost some weight. That's the trouble with guinea-pigs. They're basically eating machines. If they run out of food they eat their bedding, and when they get through that they

eat anything else they can get their teeth into.'

'*Eating machines!*' Olga wished she could join in the conversation, but as her mouth was full of paper at the time all she could manage was a gurgle. She could have told Mr Sawdust a thing or two. 'What's wrong with that?' she would have said. Just because she'd happened to tear a strip off his newspaper that morning, there was no need to go on about it. It wasn't her fault it happened to be his best bit— the part with something called a crossword on it. He shouldn't have let it fall on the floor. It hadn't tasted very nice anyway, and she'd only eaten enough to keep her going until her own breakfast came. As for eating the clue to twenty-three across, whatever that was, how was she to know?

That night Olga stayed awake long after the Sawdust family had gone to bed, and when she did eventually fall asleep it was only to dream she was being chased by a whole army of calories. Great big things they were, with long arms, huge flapping wings, and not a scrap of fur to be seen anywhere.

She had no idea what time it was when she woke, but the house was quiet and the last of the

clicks and squeaks and whirring noises had long since died away.

Olga lay where she was for a while, turning the whole thing over in her mind. It was all very well Noel saying it wouldn't last. How long was that? To take her mind off the matter she looked for a particularly large blade of grass she had been saving in case she got hungry in the night, but although she could smell it, she couldn't find it anywhere, so in the end she gave up. It seemed to her that if the Sawdust family had stopped eating their calories, then somewhere or other there must be a whole store full of them just waiting to be eaten, and she set off to see what she could find.

The only thing that worried her was that she might meet Noel. It wasn't that she didn't trust him, but he did have a habit of licking his lips sometimes, and looking over his shoulder to see if anyone else was around. She wasn't sure that she wanted to bump into him at night when he was 'doing his rounds', especially if he was on a diet too.

Sniffing her way round the room, she felt the warmth from the hot water pipes and made sure she didn't get too close in case she burnt her nose. Working her way in and out of some chair legs, she made her way towards the kitchen.

Her heart began to beat faster, for she never went anywhere near that part of the house. She'd tried it once, but that had been in broad daylight, and she had found the floor much too slippery for her liking.

Suddenly, just as she was edging her way past the door leading to the garden, she heard a movement from somewhere overhead. It was followed by a shaft of light from an upstairs window, then the sound of a door being closed.

'Wheeeeee!' she squeaked, as she turned on her heels. 'Wheeeeeeeeeee!' Then 'Wheeee! Wheeeeeee! Wheeeeeeeeeee!' as she felt her feet begin to slide on the tiles, followed by an even louder 'Wheeeeeeeughhh!' as she skidded and hit her nose on something hard, which turned out to be the stool.

21

She had only just reached the safety of her
box when there was a loud bang from the
direction of the pussy flap and Noel came
running into the house.

'Are you all right?' he gasped. 'I heard your
cries. They sounded funny.'

'I've hurt my nose,' said Olga.

'Is that all?' Noel looked disappointed.
'With a nose that size it's a wonder you don't do
it more often.'

Olga forgot the pain for
a moment. 'I should be
careful,' she warned. 'Mr
Sawdust might catch you
and wonder what you've
been up to.'

'It's all right,' said Noel. 'He's gone out jogging. At least, he calls it jogging, but if you ask me I think he goes out to get something to eat because when he gets back he always says he feels better for it.'

'Perhaps,' said Olga, anxious to change the subject of her accident, 'he wants to have a wonderful figure like mine.'

Noel stared at her. 'When did you ever do any jogging?' he asked.

'Guinea-pigs do it all the time,' said Olga primly. 'Only we don't bother going out to do it. We call it "jogging on the spot". I don't suppose you've ever noticed me doing it, because being as light as a feather you can't hear me, and when I get going it's so fast you wouldn't have been able to see it.

'Then again, some guinea-pigs only do it at night. If you're ever out and you hear a sound like snowflakes falling, it's probably a passing guinea-pig having a midnight jog on the way home.'

'Snowflakes!' said Noel disbelievingly. 'Midnight jogs!'

Olga gave a deep sigh. Noel wasn't the best audience in the world. 'I was going to tell you a story,' she said. 'But if you don't want to hear it . . .'

Olga knew better than to wait for a reply. She plunged straight in before Noel had a chance to open his mouth.

'It's about the days when guinea-pigs were worshipped even more than they are today—if you can picture such a thing. The most famous guinea-pig of all was known as Olga the Great. She was the biggest and most beautiful pig the world had ever seen.

'She was also very wise. In fact she was so wise she didn't have room in her head for all the things she knew, so she kept most of the best bits in her nose, which became bigger and bigger as time went on.

'Her nose grew so big that when she breathed out it was like a soft and gentle wind blowing across all the land.'

'What happened when she snored?' asked Noel. 'Did it wake everyone up? I expect they all ran for cover.'

'Guinea-pigs don't snore,' said Olga crossly. 'I know because I stayed awake one night to see if I did, and I didn't!'

She took the opportunity to look for the blade of grass again, but she still couldn't see it anywhere, so she carried on with her story.

'As I was saying, Olga the Great had the biggest, most wonderful nose in the whole, wide world, and it was covered in the softest fur you could possibly imagine. Stroking it was considered a great honour, second only to touching her whiskers, which were so long they had to be propped up, for they went on and on until they disappeared over the edge of the

world and when the wind blew it made a sound like a thousand violins being played.

'On hot days other animals would travel long distances to rest under the shade of her nose and nibble the wonderful grass that grew there. Afterwards they played games until it grew dark and it was time to go home.'

'What happened to her?' demanded Noel, who in spite of himself was hanging on Olga's every word. 'I've never seen anything like that round here.'

Olga went quiet for a moment. It wasn't the first time she had let her imagination run away with her. It sometimes happened when she was telling a story.

'It was in a faraway land,' she said at last. 'And cats weren't allowed in.' She gave a sigh. 'Such beauty was too much for one guinea-pig to deal with all by herself, so in the end she did the only thing possible. She sent others out into the world to carry on the work for her. Of course, she had to be very strict about it. Only the best quality pigs were allowed to take the work on.

The ones with the softest fur, the longest whiskers, and the most beautiful noses. Which is really how I came to be here . . .'

Noel arched his back and gave a snort; the one he kept for when he'd had enough of something. 'I haven't noticed any other guinea-pigs walking miles to rest under *your* nose,' he said. 'Or have a go at eating any of your grass. The chance would be a fine thing.'

'It's here when they want it,' said Olga stiffly. 'They have only to ask.'

But she was suddenly tired out by all her story telling. Tired out and hungry. Besides, it was starting to get light and it would soon be time for breakfast. Somewhere or other she knew she had a lovely, succulent blade she had been saving until later. She could smell it and her mouth was beginning to water at the thought.

'If I were you,' said Noel, as he stalked off, 'I should try looking nearer home.'

Cats! thought Olga, as he disappeared. They must always have the last word.

She stepped back a pace, and as she did so she discovered a very annoying thing. Noel was right after all. There was the blade of grass she had been looking for; under the end of her nose!

3

The Night Olga Nearly Met Father Christmas

If Olga thought her early morning ramble would go unnoticed she was mistaken. The very first thing Mrs Sawdust saw when she came downstairs was a trail of wood shavings and bits of hay leading from her box right round the dining-room and into the kitchen.

'She must have been sleepwalking,' said Karen Sawdust.

'But she never goes into the kitchen,' said Mrs Sawdust. 'Not even when she's awake.'

'There's always a first time for everything,' said Mr Sawdust. 'I expect she was looking for something to eat,' he continued, putting his finger on the problem. 'And I can't say I blame her.'

Olga wasn't the only one who was getting fed up with being on a diet. That evening, when he came home from the office, Mr Sawdust brought with him several packets labelled *Carrot Slims*.

'We'll see what Olga makes of these if she can get her teeth into them,' he said. 'I know

what it's like to get hungry in the night and we'd never forgive ourselves if anything happened to her.'

Mrs Sawdust opened one of the packets and felt inside. 'I don't know about getting her teeth into them,' she said. 'I only hope she can get them out again.'

'Carrot *slims*! That's a laugh!' said Noel, when he heard about it. 'I wondered what all the noise was about. It's worse than when everyone had toast for breakfast. At least they didn't carry on eating it all day long.'

He stared at Olga as she picked one up in her teeth and began crunching. 'They don't seem to be working very well,' he said.

'I'm only on my first box,' said Olga, '*crunch, crunch*. Just you wait. I might disappear through a crack in the floor one of these days, *crunch, crunch*. Then you'll be sorry, *crunch, crunch*.'

'Huh!' said Noel, and having failed to have the last word he went out into the garden for a bit of peace and quiet.

But as it happened, matters came to a head a few days later when Mr Sawdust returned from his morning run and went into the kitchen for a glass of water. Creeping through the dining-room in the semi-dark with no shoes on, he happened to tread on one of Olga's Carrot Slims. His cry of agony was worse than all Olga's past squeaks put together. Worse still, when he switched the light on he found that most of the crumbs—the ones that weren't stuck to his foot—were ground into the carpet, and he had to get the vacuum cleaner out to clear up the mess.

The unusual noise at that hour of the morning woke everyone else.

'That settles it,' said Mrs Sawdust. 'No more dieting for a while! Bacon and eggs, anyone?'

Her words brought sighs of relief all round, not least from Olga, who was only too keen to make up for lost time. Carrot Slims were very nice in their place, but they did make her jaws ache. Even Mr Sawdust had remarked that by now her jaws must be so strong they would come in very useful for doing odd jobs about the house.

'Anyway,' said Karen Sawdust, as she left for school, 'it's only four weeks until Christmas, so we shall have to go into training for all the mince pies.'

Olga stopped eating and pricked up her ears. 'Only four "Wheeks" until Christmas!' she repeated. 'Wheeeeeeek! Wheeeeeeeek! Wheeeeeeeeeeeek!'

She still remembered Christmas from last year. It was the first time she had been allowed to spend nearly all day in the Sawdust family's house and there had been lots of parcels to open. Afterwards there had been games and goodness knows what else. Karen Sawdust had made a tunnel for her out of some building blocks, and altogether she'd had a lovely time.

Her cries reached Noel in the garden. 'What's going on?' he cried, as he came indoors. 'Have I missed something?'

'It's only four "Wheeeeks" to Christmas,' said Olga, 'and I've done three "Wheeeeks" already, so it must be nearly here. It's a good job I've been practising my eating, otherwise I'd have to go into training like the others.'

'Is that all?' said Noel. 'You want to watch out. The way you're carrying on you might get stuck in your box and miss Christmas altogether.'

'And you want to watch out you don't eat so much you get stuck in your pussy flap and the back half of you has to spend it in the garden,' said Olga, not to be outdone.

Noel turned his back on her in disgust, but it was noticeable that until Mrs Sawdust sent him packing, he hung around the kitchen in case there was any cream going spare.

'Animals!' she said that evening over dinner. 'I'll swear some of them know more about what's going on than is good for them.'

Gradually over the next few weeks 'things began to happen' in the Sawdust household. Every time the postman called he brought cards, which were pinned to tapes hanging down the wall.

Then one day Mr Sawdust arrived home carrying a large tree, which he decorated with coloured lights that flashed on and off.

Olga gazed in wonder at the sight. There were so many she couldn't even begin to count them, and whenever she tried they went out again.

'I think we're in for a white Christmas,' said Noel that afternoon when he came in from the garden. 'My whiskers are sticking out, and that's usually a sign it's going to snow.'

And sure enough, give Noel his due, for he did know about these things, shortly afterwards white flakes began falling from the sky. Soon everything in the garden became covered with a thick blanket of snow.

Karen Sawdust spent the evening sitting at the dining-room table staring at Olga and from time to time writing things down on a piece of paper.

Afterwards, just before she went to bed, she put the paper in the fireplace alongside a plate of biscuits and mince pies.

As soon as they were on their own Noel gave the plate a sniff. 'I don't like mince pies,' he said. 'Never did. You'd think they'd have left some cream out for Father Christmas, though. I expect he likes cream.'

Olga had a sniff too, and she had to agree with Noel about mince pies. 'Who's Father Christmas?' she asked. 'Is he coming to stay?'

'Father Christmas doesn't *stay* anywhere,' said Noel, anxious to air his knowledge. 'He's much too busy. No one ever sees him. He goes round all the houses leaving presents. Karen Sawdust says that if you're very lucky you get all the things you wished for.'

Olga decided to stay awake that night in the hope that she might see Father Christmas for herself. But what with one thing and another, although she did remember half waking up at one point, it seemed as though no sooner had she closed her eyes than it was daylight again.

She looked around the room and lo and behold, there in the fireplace was a small pile of parcels, all done up in brightly coloured paper tied with ribbon. *And* all the biscuits had gone!

She gave a squeak of delight. 'Wheeeeeeee! Father Christmas has been and gone and I nearly saw him. I would have done if I'd stayed awake. He must have been very quiet . . . He's left the mince pie, but he's eaten all the biscuits.'

She broke off. For a moment she thought she saw the suspicion of a crumb on Noel's whiskers. But he was too quick for her. His tongue went in and out like greased lightning.

And what parcels they were!

Noel had a tin of his favourite cat food and a small carton of cream, and Olga had a bundle of mixed vegetables: carrots, French beans, and broccoli, all wrapped in lettuce leaves to keep them moist.

'Wheeeeeeeee!' she squeaked. 'What a nice man Father Christmas must be. He thinks of everything and he knows just what people like best.'

Much later that day, when the Sawdust family sat down to dinner, Mr Sawdust raised his glass. 'Here's to absent friends,' he said. To which everyone else added a loud 'Hear! Hear!'

It made Olga think of Graham and Fangio, still fast asleep. Graham, packed away in the summer-house in case he dug himself in somewhere, which he was apt to do when it got cold and no one was looking; and Fangio in one of his many hideaways. (Nobody knew which of the many he had built himself in the garden, and he never, ever, let on.)

Fancy never seeing Christmas, thought

Olga. I'm glad I'm not a tortoise or a hedgehog.

Then the sight of everyone else eating gave her an idea. She gave herself two extra helpings of her present; one for each of them. It was her good turn for Christmas and she felt much better about them afterwards.

4

A Lick and a Promise

One Saturday morning in early spring Karen
Sawdust came down to breakfast and asked
what date it was.

Mr Sawdust looked at his newspaper. 'It's
the 18th,' he said. 'Why do you ask?'

'I was thinking in bed last night,' said
Karen, 'isn't it time Graham was up? It's gone
half past March and he's usually awake by now.
Fangio's been around for several weeks. I've
heard rustling in the bushes.'

'Hedgehogs are more regular,' said Mr Sawdust. 'Fangio always puts himself to bed without fail on October the first. Graham didn't go to bed until much nearer the end of the month.'

'It was the twenty-second of October,' said Mrs Sawdust. 'I looked it up only yesterday. Mind you, the mornings are quite dark still. Perhaps he's overslept. We'll have a look when we've finished eating.'

And sure enough, after breakfast Karen and Mrs Sawdust returned from a trip to the summer-house carrying a very sleepy-looking tortoise.

Olga hadn't realized getting Graham up involved quite so much work, and she watched with interest. First of all he had to have a bath, then Mrs Sawdust brought out some old scales and weighed him.

Afterwards she counted the rings on his shell. 'He'll be forty years old this year,' she said. 'And he weighs 1740 grams. Let's see . . .' she checked in her notebook, '. . . when he went

to bed last year he weighed 1765 grams. That means he's only lost 25 grams in the twenty-one weeks he's been asleep. He's lived on his reserves all that time.'

'An example to us all,' said Mr Sawdust looking pointedly at Olga.

I wonder what he meant by that? thought Olga. There was no telling with the Sawdust people at times. She certainly wasn't going without food all the winter to please anyone. As for living on her 'reserves'—she hoped it would never come to that.

After Graham was safely installed in his house at the bottom of the garden, with fresh newspaper on the floor and plenty of hay in case the nights were chilly, Mrs Sawdust began putting food out at night for Fangio. A few evenings later they were rewarded by the sound of clanking dishes outside the back door, and afterwards when they looked out of the window a shadowy figure could be seen scurrying off into the bushes.

If March was the time of the Great Awakening, it was also the month of the Great Misunderstanding.

It happened one Sunday. Karen was staying with a friend, and Mrs Sawdust had to go out,

leaving Mr Sawdust to get his own lunch.

'It's all right,' she said, when she caught him looking in the refrigerator. 'You'll not starve. We'll make up for it tonight when I get back.'

'I know I shan't starve,' said Mr Sawdust. 'It's just the principle of the thing. I paid a lot of money for this refrigerator—it was the biggest they had in the shop—and look at it! As far as I can see Fangio's got half the crisper section. Graham's got the other half and Olga's been given two whole shelves—the best ones at that —for all her bits and pieces. Noel's got the next one up. It would be nice if I didn't have to grope around on the top shelf for what's left. It makes me feel like a second class citizen.'

'The difference is,' said Mrs Sawdust firmly, 'you can help yourself whenever you like. The others have to wait for someone to get it for them.

'Yours is in a plastic pot marked "S" for Stew. I've peeled some potatoes—they're in another pot next to it. And there are some peas in the freezer.'

As the voices died away Olga went back to her washing. It was all very interesting, but if she wasn't careful she might forget where she'd got to and go over the same spot twice by mistake, which would never do.

Towards the end of the morning she was woken by a click as the refrigerator door was opened, and after a short pause she heard the sound of things happening in the kitchen; saucepans clattering and taps running, followed by a pop as the stove was lit. It wasn't long before familiar smells began wafting in her direction.

Olga sniffed. Oh dear, she thought.

She gave a warning squeak: 'Wheeeee!'

'Don't worry, old girl,' said Mr Sawdust, 'I haven't forgotten you.' And he brought her a large pile of grass.

Old girl! thought Olga. 'Grass! I don't want any grass—well, not just yet anyway! Wheeeeeeeeee!' It was out of her mouth before she realized what she had just said. Shortly after that Mr Sawdust brought her some carrots to go with the grass.

The unexpected windfall kept her going until he came back into the room carrying his lunch on a plate. The smell was even stronger close to.

Oh dear, oh dear, she thought. There was only one thing for it. Taking a deep breath, she lifted up her head and gave one of her loudest ever warning cries.

'Wheeeeeeeeeeeeeeeeeeeeeeeeeeeeeeeeeeeeee!'

Mr Sawdust put down his plate and stared at her. 'Don't tell me you're still hungry?' he said. And he brought her some lettuce leaves.

Olga gave another squeak, and as squeak followed squeak, so beans, broccoli, carrots, and beetroot appeared in quick succession, until he gave up the battle.

Oh, well, thought Olga as she tucked in, nobody could say I haven't done my best.

She hadn't seen so much food for a long time and, as for Mr Sawdust, he enjoyed his lunch so much he went into the kitchen to get some bread in order to wipe his plate clean.

It was late that afternoon before Karen and Mrs Sawdust arrived back. As soon as they had taken their coats off Karen went down on her knees to say hello to Olga, while Mrs Sawdust went to the refrigerator to get something for tea.

'Oh, dear,' she called. 'I don't think your father ate the stew I left for him.'

'I certainly did,' said Mr Sawdust, as he came into the room. 'And very tasty it was, too. Best I've had for a long time.'

'Thank you *very* much,' said Mrs Sawdust drily. 'I must get some more tins of it next time I'm in the pet shop.'

'The *pet* shop?' repeated Mr Sawdust. 'What do you mean?'

Mrs Sawdust held up an empty container.

'You ate the cat food by mistake!'

Olga looked from one to the other as they talked. 'Wheeeee!' she squeaked. 'I tried to tell you, only you wouldn't listen.'

Mr Sawdust seemed to go a funny shade of green. 'The cat food!' he repeated. 'What did it have in it?'

'I don't know, dear,' said Mrs Sawdust. 'You'd better ask Noel. It was his favourite. He ate half of it yesterday and I was saving the rest for him to have tonight as a treat. He won't be too pleased when he hears it's all gone!'

'*He* won't be too pleased,' exclaimed Mr Sawdust. 'I like that! What about me?'

'You said it was the best stew you've had for a long time.'

'That was before I knew what it was,' replied Mr Sawdust.

Mrs Sawdust pointed to the container lid. 'I did tell you yours was marked with an "S" for stew. You took the one marked with an "N" for Noel. It was one of his overflows.'

Mr Sawdust stared at the object in her hand.

'It looks like an "S" to me.'

'It depends which way you look at it,' said Mrs Sawdust, turning it round. 'I was in a bit of a hurry when I did it.'

There was no knowing how long the argument might have gone on for, but at that very moment there was a bang from the direction of the kitchen and Noel himself came into the dining-room licking his lips.

'Will you tell him?' said Mrs Sawdust, 'or shall I?'

Noel gave a loud 'Miaaooow' when he saw the empty pot.

'Just you watch it!' said Mr Sawdust. He gave a groan. 'That does it! I feel sick. I'm going upstairs to lie down.'

As he left the room Noel wrapped himself round Mrs Sawdust's legs and gave a hopeful purr. 'Oh, dear,' she said. 'I feel like a murderess. A double one at that!'

Olga retired to her room.

One way and another it looked as though they were in for an unhappy evening.

Mr Sawdust held his breath as Olga climbed down off the duvet and inched her way along his chest. As she leant forward he could feel her whiskers tickling his chin and it made him want to sneeze, but he didn't dare in case it made her jump and she fell off the bed.

He wouldn't have said it out loud, for fear that something in his tone of voice might hurt her feelings, but her tongue did feel rather rough. It was not unlike a tiny piece of sandpaper; the very best quality, of course, but there was no getting away from the fact that it put him in mind of sandpaper.

'You're very honoured,' said Mrs Sawdust, as Karen picked Olga up and gave her a hug. 'She doesn't kiss just anyone, and then only when she feels like it.'

Mr Sawdust sat up. 'You know,' he said, 'it's a very strange thing, but I think I feel better already. I may come downstairs for dinner after all.'

Mrs Sawdust gave a sigh of relief. 'Thank goodness for that,' she said. 'I was beginning to feel quite worried.'

'I don't think it's strange at all,' said Karen. 'I think we should say thank you to nurse Polga. There's nothing like a guinea-pig's lick to make a person feel on top of the world. It's a bit like being knighted by the Queen. You can't ever ask for it, but that makes it all the more precious when it happens.'

5

The Tale of the Magical Conch Shell

With the coming of spring Olga was able to meet up again with Graham and Fangio—both of whom were out and about now they had recovered from their long winter sleep.

Most afternoons when it was sunny she had tea on the lawn. Nice though it was to be living in a big house as a member of the family, a part of her longed for the wide open spaces. Not too

wide, of course, and not too open, for fear other animals might take a fancy to her when she was looking the other way.

There had been rumours of a fox having been seen in the neighbourhood, so having the protection of her portable run with its wire-netting top and sides was ideal. It not only meant she could keep the others entertained with her stories while she ate, but Mr Sawdust was pleased because it saved him having to mow the lawn quite so often.

Not that Olga spent all her spare time eating

and telling stories. Sometimes, when the sun was high in the sky, she retired to the shelter of the boarded-in part of the run in order to enjoy a bit of peace and quiet and a well-earned rest. Telling stories could be very tiring, especially when you had a mouth full of grass.

Then one day, she came out of her box after a nap and had a terrible shock. At the top of some steps leading down off the lawn to the patio outside the house, there was a very strange object. It was like nothing she had ever seen before and it certainly hadn't been there before she went to sleep. It was almost as big as Noel, but round and shiny—and with a big hole towards one end.

'Wheeeeeee!' she shrieked. 'Wheeeeeeee! Wheeeeeeeee! Wheeeeeeeeeeeee!' Her cries brought the others running.

Noel was first on the scene and he didn't look best pleased at being woken up when he saw what all the fuss was about.

'Have you finished?' he asked. 'Have you quite finished? It's only a conch shell.'

Olga peered out of her run. 'A conch shell?' she repeated. 'What's it for?'

'It's not *for* anything,' said Noel. 'I expect Mr Sawdust bought it to decorate the garden. I saw him blowing into it this morning. He made a honking noise with it. Then I heard him telling Karen Sawdust a story about how if you put your ear to the hole you can sometimes hear the sea. I daresay—' Noel broke off as he put one of his own ears to the shell. 'Ssh! Be quiet!'

'I wasn't saying anything,' exclaimed Olga, looking most offended.

'Well, would you believe it?' said Noel. 'Would you believe it?'

'I might if you told me,' said Olga crossly. She wasn't used to others taking over her role as storyteller in chief.

'I don't know about the sea,' said Noel. 'It sounds like a lot of guinea-pigs to me. They must be having a picnic. You've never heard such a din.' He took his head out of the opening and licked his lips. 'It's so real you can almost taste the sandwiches.'

'Sandwiches!' said Olga crossly, as she munched away at the grass. 'That's all you ever think about . . . food!'

'Listen to who's talking,' said Noel. 'I'm going back to sleep. Who wants to listen to a lot of guinea-pigs chattering away?'

'Quite a lot of people I would imagine,' said Olga stiffly. 'I expect if it was on television it would be very popular. Everybody likes to watch guinea-pigs enjoying themselves. Not that it happens very often when there are cats around,' she added. But she was talking to herself, for Noel had already disappeared the way he had come.

Graham was next on the scene, puffing his way up the ramp Mr Sawdust had made so that he could reach the lawn. 'Are you all right?' he called. 'I hope I'm not too late. I've been as quick as I can.'

'I'm safe and well, thank you very much,' said Olga.

Graham's head appeared at the top of the ramp and there was a pause while he hauled the

rest of himself up the last few centimetres.

'What's that big round thing?' he said. 'It's in my way.'

'Don't *you* start,' said Olga. 'It's only a conch shell.'

'A conch shell?' repeated Graham, as he carried on walking. Graham not only thought he had right of way, but he took the view that the shortest distance between two points was a straight line.

A moment later there was a heavy clonk, not unlike the sound of two coconuts being banged together. It took him a little while to recover, but slowly his head emerged from inside his own shell and he took a closer look.

'Well I never!' he cried. 'That's funny. There's music coming out of it.'

'*Music?*' repeated Olga, interested in spite of herself. 'What else can you hear?'

'Well, there's the sea,' said Graham. 'And an aeroplane going over. And an ice-cream van. Oooh, I'm off to my pool for a bathe. It's just what I fancy. There's nothing like a bathe on a hot day. I bet you wish you could come too, stuck in a run like that.'

'I'm happy where I am, thank you very much,' said Olga, pretending she hadn't a care in the world. 'There's a lovely breeze blowing through my whiskers.'

But her peace and quiet didn't last very long, for no sooner had Graham disappeared

than she heard a familiar grunting and rustling in the shrubbery and Fangio appeared.

'*Mama Mia!*' he cried, when he saw the conch shell.

Olga gave a loud sigh. Now what? she thought.

'You know something?' said Fangio, as he peered inside the opening. 'I can hear a band playing. I think it's coming from this thingamajig. I knew something was keeping me awake this morning. I was in the middle of a dream all about a lake that was made of bread and milk.'

'I know a story about a lake,' broke in Olga. 'It belonged to a beautiful guinea-pig princess who lived in a nearby castle . . .'

'I'm sorry,' said Fangio. 'Some other time. I have to go.'

Olga felt very flat when Fangio disappeared. She looked round the garden, but everything had gone quiet again. Venables, the toad, was nowhere in sight and even the goldfish were hiding somewhere. There was just no one to talk to.

Oh, if only I could see inside a conch shell, she thought. If cats and tortoises and hedgehogs can hear all the things they say they can, just think what a guinea-pig would be able to hear. I'd be able to tell the most wonderful stories.

As it happened, Olga's chance came sooner than she expected. The very next morning, while she was waiting for Mrs Sawdust to finish cleaning out her box, she went round the dining-room on a tour of inspection and noticed a cupboard door had been left open. Mrs Sawdust had gone outside to empty the dustpan, so for the moment she was on her own. Seizing the opportunity, she peeped round the door and as she did so her heart nearly missed a beat, for there, lying on the floor in front of her, lay the conch shell.

'Now wheeee shall see,' she squeaked, hurrying into the cupboard as fast as her legs would carry her.

She put one ear to the shell and listened, then she tried shaking it, but there was nothing;

absolutely nothing. She almost plucked up the
courage to climb inside, but then thought better
of it in case she got stuck. Instead she stared at
it in disgust. She had never seen or heard so
much nothing in her whole life.

'What are you doing in there?' called Noel,
looking in through the window. 'What's going
on?'

'Never you mind,' said Olga crossly. 'It's
none of your business.'

And with that she found a dark corner of the
cupboard, clear of his prying eyes and waited
until all was quiet again.

The most that anyone saw of Olga for the rest of that day was her back view as she hid in her hay. She couldn't tell the others that nothing had happened. She would never hear the last of it. But try as she might she couldn't think up a story . . .

. . . until the next day when she was out on the lawn again.

She happened to glance up and there it was again. Only this time the conch shell was standing on the edge of the fishpond.

But it was very different to the way she remembered it. Overnight the Sawdust family must have been working on it, for the inside had been turned into a miniature garden, full of tiny flowers and trees. There was even a tiny path leading to a bridge across a stream, and from there on to goodness only knew where.

'Wheeee!' she shrieked. 'Wheeeeee! Wheeeeeeeeee! WHEEEEEEEEEE!'

Once again all the other animals came running.

'Don't worry,' called Graham. 'Hold on! I'm coming!'

'So that's what you were doing in the cupboard!' said Noel, who got there just before him. 'Making a garden. Hmm. Not bad. Not bad at all.'

Olga gave a start. Then she seized her opportunity. 'Oh, er, it was nothing,' she said. 'It's the kind of thing we guinea-pigs do all the time.'

'It's magic!' cried Fangio, woken from his slumbers once again. 'That's what it is—it's magic!'

'If you like,' said Olga, 'I may even tell you a story about it . . . later on . . . when I've thought one up . . . er . . . I mean . . .'

'Don't start yet,' said Fangio. 'I'm going to form a queue.'

'Wait for me,' called Graham.

'I'm first,' said Noel. 'I'm first.'

'You'll have to wait,' said Olga. 'I must finish this patch of grass before I do anything else. You can't tell stories on an empty stomach.'

She took another look at the conch shell. Fangio was right. It did have a magical look about it. In fact, it would be a very good name for her story. She would call it *The Tale of the Magical Conch Shell*.

But it had taught her one thing. 'I shall never, ever boast again,' she decided. 'And I expect my "not boasting" will be the best "not boasting" that has ever been known in the whole of the world!'

6
An Unwelcome Visitor

It was Noel who brought the news. He always liked to be the first to know what was going on and he couldn't wait to tell the others. The bang from his pussy flap echoed round the patio as he scrambled through and ran out of the house.

'There's someone coming to stay,' he panted. 'I've just heard Mrs Sawdust talking on the telephone. Whoever it is they talk a lot, and they're on their way.'

'That sounds like Wayne,' said Fangio, turning round so that he was facing the way he

68

had come. 'If it's Wayne, I'm off. The last time he came to stay he tried using me as a football.'

'Wait for me!' called Graham. 'He's always wanting me to stick my head out of my shell when I don't want to. The last time he was here he poked a stick down inside and he couldn't get it out again. I had to chew the end off it before I could see out.'

Graham could show a surprising turn of speed when he felt like it, and before Olga had time to reply he was off down the garden path and disappearing up the ramp leading into his house as though his very life depended on it.

'Wayne's always trying to stroke me,' said Olga, who until that moment had been enjoying the sunshine in her run on the lawn. 'I can understand it, of course, guinea-pig's fur being so soft and inviting, but I'm frightened he'll poke a finger in my eye one of these days. Besides, his hands are always sticky.'

'I expect it saves using a towel,' said Noel unfeelingly, as he came alongside her. 'Besides, your fur's not much to write home about anyway.' Noel wasn't sure what that meant, but he liked showing off and he'd heard Mr Sawdust use the expression from time to time when he didn't fancy something. 'It's not like my tail. If he's not careful he'll pull it off one of these days and that would be much worse.'

'I expect he thinks he's doing you a good turn,' said Olga, not wishing to be outdone. 'I expect he thinks you'll be glad to be rid of it, hanging there all day doing nothing.'

'Doing nothing!' exclaimed Noel. 'Doing nothing! I'll have you know it does all sorts of things. It keeps the flies away for a start.'

'I expect you could do with that,' said Olga. 'I've noticed you always get a lot round you in the hot weather.'

Noel arched his back. 'I also use it to dust places before I sit down,' he said. 'Cats are very particular about these things. Not like pigs. Pigs lie down anywhere.'

With that he stalked back into the house to await developments.

Olga helped herself to one more mouthful

from the lawn, then she made her way into the room at the end of her run. If Wayne was coming to stay, she didn't want to take any chances, although she made sure she was still within nibbling distance of any stray blades of grass that happened to be sticking up in case she was there a long time. There was no sense in going hungry.

Everything in the garden had gone quiet. The only sound came from the fountain in the nearby pool, and because it was warm inside the box, she soon fell fast asleep.

Olga had no idea how long she slept, but she was in the middle of a particularly nice dream, all about living in a house where everything, even the carpet, was covered in grass, and the table legs weren't wood at all, but were made out of carrots and beans, when she woke to the sound of a voice coming from somewhere nearby.

'Who's a pretty girl then?' it asked.

Olga blinked herself awake and gave a squeak. 'I am, of course,' she replied sleepily.

71

Thinking it was a silly question to ask, she looked out of her run to see where the voice was coming from, but the garden still seemed deserted. All she could hear was the sound of birds chirruping from nearby trees, as though they had taken fright at something, so she closed her eyes again.

The next moment she was cowering in the back of her run thinking her last moment had come.

She lay still for a moment or two, hardly daring to breathe. Never in the whole of her life had she heard such a din. First of all, Noel—and she knew at once that it had to be him, it couldn't have been anyone else—Noel let out such an agonized cry it made her blood run cold.

No sooner had his pussy flap slammed shut behind him as he shot back into the house, than she heard the sound of voices and people running.

Olga gave a sigh as she ventured into her run and peered out through the wire netting.

Why was it that some of the best things in life happened where you couldn't quite see them?

'You can't blame Polly,' she heard Mrs Sawdust say. 'It's in her nature. If you ask me Noel must have put his head too near her cage.'

'Cats who aren't able to mind their own business must expect to lose a whisker or two,' agreed Karen Sawdust. 'All the same, I bet it was painful. I wouldn't like to have a parrot wrap one of my whiskers round its beak and give it a tug.'

A parrot? thought Olga. Whatever can she mean? And she went straight back inside her room again in case her own whiskers met with the same fate as Noel's.

Olga had never even heard of a parrot before, let alone seen one, and she wasn't sure what to expect when later that day she was taken indoors. She certainly hadn't pictured it being a bird; at least she supposed it was a bird, for it had two legs and it was clinging to the roof bars of a large cage standing on the Sawdust family's dining-room table. But it was like no other bird she had ever seen before. It was much bigger and brightly coloured for a start,

and it kept staring at her through two unblinking beady eyes. She was glad it wasn't flying around loose.

Plucking up courage, she gave a small 'Wheee!'

'Wheee!' said the bird in return.

Olga looked round to make sure she had heard aright. It was something else she had never come across before; a bird with a guinea-pig's voice. She tried again.

'Wheeeee! Wheeeee!'

'Wheeeee! Wheeeee!' The parrot bobbed its head up and down with excitement. 'Wheeeeeeee! Wheeeeeeee! Wheeeeeeee!'

Yes, well, thought Olga. It's quite good for a

bird, I suppose . . . even if it doesn't make sense, but it's not as good as the real thing. That would be too much to expect. And she gave several more 'wheeee's' just to show what they really should sound like.

The parrot put her head on one side to listen, then tried again, only much louder this time. Louder and harsher; more of a squawk than a squeak. Olga almost began to wish she hadn't started it.

'I shouldn't get too close if I were you,' said Noel, as he came into the room. He looked a bit put out to find Olga talking to the parrot. 'She had one of my whiskers. I shall have to be careful until it grows again. No going through gaps in a hurry in case I get stuck.'

Olga wasn't one to miss an opportunity. 'That's what comes of eating so much,' she said, looking up from her bowl of oats. 'It's a wonder you get through any gaps at all you're so fat.'

Noel stared at her as if he could hardly believe his ears. 'Hark who's talking! At least I don't eat paper.'

'Paper?' repeated Olga.

'I've heard you,' said Noel. 'Tearing up paper in the night when you think no one else is around. Mr Sawdust is always grumbling when he finds bits missing.'

'That's different,' said Olga primly.

'I'll say it's different,' said Noel. 'Mmmmmmeeaaawscrunchhhh! Parrots aren't the only ones who copy the sounds others make, you know.'

Noel's impression of Olga's paper tearing sounded as though he had swallowed a large bumble bee which had got itself stuck halfway down his throat.

Even the parrot, having had several goes at trying to imitate it, gave up in disgust.

Olga tried tearing a piece out of the piece of newspaper she was standing on to show Noel it was nothing like the noise he had just made. But he was clearly so pleased with himself he went around the house for the rest of the day repeating it whenever he got the chance.

In the end Mrs Sawdust couldn't stand it a moment longer.

'There's something terribly wrong with him,' she said, when Mr Sawdust came home from work. 'I think he must have a fishbone stuck in his throat. Though where he got it from goodness only knows. We haven't had any fish for days.'

'Somebody else's dustbin I expect,' said Mr Sawdust.

Mrs Sawdust waited until Noel was in the kitchen, then she made a grab. Before he had a chance to escape he was inside his travelling basket with the lid tightly shut. 'It's off to the vet with you, my lad,' she said. 'We'll get you X-rayed.'

Noel peered mournfully at Olga through a grille in the side of the basket.

'Did you hear that?' he miaowed. 'You know what that means? They're going to look inside my stomach to see what they can find.'

'Weeeeeugh!' squeaked Olga. 'I expect it's full of mice.'

'If they looked inside yours,' said Noel, 'there's no knowing what they would find. It must be packed tight with all sorts of things. Grass and oats and carrots and hay and beans and . . . and bits of paper.'

'Mmmmmeeaaawwscreeunchhh!' he miaowed crossly, as he was carried away. 'This is all your fault.'

'Wheeeeeeee!' said Olga. 'All my fault. I like that!'

'Wheeeeeeeee!' squawked the parrot. 'All

my fault. I like that! Wheeeeee! Wheeeee! Wheeeeeee!'

'Dear, oh dear,' said Mr Sawdust. 'It's worse than being in a zoo!'

'Dear, oh dear,' squawked the parrot. 'It's worse than being in a zoo.'

'Wheeeeee!' said Olga, half to herself as they were left alone together. 'You wouldn't think one bird could make so much noise.'

'Wheeeeeeeeee!' repeated the parrot. 'Wheeeeee! Wheeeeeeee! Wheeeeeeeee!'

And there was worse to come. It wasn't long before Olga wished she had never opened her mouth.

By the time the Sawdust family got back the house was in an uproar, with Olga and the parrot going at each other hammer and tongs.

'I can't stand too much of this,' said Mr Sawdust. 'It's bad enough having Olga shrieking her head off when it's meal-time, but this is too much of a good thing.'

'I can't think what's come over them both,' agreed Mrs Sawdust. 'It used to be such a quiet house. It's a good job Noel isn't here. The vet couldn't find anything, so he's being kept in under observation for a while in case he does it again.'

'She'll have to go.'

Olga's heart missed a beat. Go? They couldn't! They wouldn't!

'What did you say, dear?' called Mrs Sawdust.

'I said "she'll have to go!"' shouted Mr Sawdust. 'That blessed parrot!'

'I'm sorry,' said Mrs Sawdust. 'I can't hear you for all the noise.'

At which point Olga gave one of her loudest and longest squeaks ever.

'Yeooowwwwweeeeeeeee!' went the parrot in return, twice as long and more than twice as loud.

And that was it, really. Mr Sawdust made a quick telephone call and, hey presto!, peace was restored.

Olga couldn't wait for Noel to get back so that she could tell him. 'It was all thanks to me,' she said proudly.

81

'Whatever did you say?' asked Noel suspiciously.

'I just gave a wheeeeee or two,' said Olga carelessly. 'Sometimes it isn't so much what guinea-pigs say, it's the way they say it!'

7

Olga and the Chinese Takeaway

Every morning, after the rest of the family had finished breakfast and Mrs Sawdust was left on her own, she always gave Olga's house a good clean before doing anything else.

'First things first,' she called it; which as far as Olga could see as she watched from a safe distance, meant relining the box with clean newspaper, sprinkling fresh sawdust on the floor, and topping up her two feeding bowls; one with clean water, the other with assorted seeds. Olga was very particular about her seeds—some disappeared down her throat like magic, others didn't receive so much as a second glance, let alone a sniff. Mr Sawdust always maintained it was any old thing they put in to make up the weight.

Next came the laying out of Olga's breakfast. Mrs Sawdust prided herself on making it look as tempting as possible. Using a lettuce leaf as a bowl, she first of all filled it with freshly cut grass from the garden; provided, of course, Mr Sawdust hadn't mown the lawn the evening before. If that happened she had to go out with her nail scissors. (Olga thought Mr Sawdust must secretly eat grass for his supper. She couldn't see any other reason for cutting it.)

This was followed by a selection of vegetables: carrots, beetroot, celery, and any others that happened to be in the shops at the time. Split down the middle, glistening with juice as they were piled on top of each other, they often looked so good Mrs Sawdust fancied

some herself. Sometimes she tried a bit when
Olga wasn't looking, eating it as quickly as
possible in case she was spotted.

Because of the juice, she always put a layer
or two of newspaper down in front of the box in
order to protect the carpet. She tried to arrange
it so that there was a nice picture to look at; a
country scene, perhaps, or something in colour,
although she was never too sure what Olga
made of them.

Being so near the ground, Olga didn't know
either. She knew they were pictures, but most of

the time she found it hard to tell exactly what they were about, and some of the best bits were usually under her nose anyway.

'Olga must be very well read by now,' said Mr Sawdust one day, when he saw her peering at a copy of yesterday's newspaper (in fact, she was looking for a seed she had dropped, but hearing her name mentioned, she automatically looked up). 'I expect she could tell a tale or two if she felt like it.'

Noel was in the room at the time and he picked up on the remark straight away.

'Huh!' he said, as soon as they were on their own. 'A tale or two! If they only knew!'

Olga pretended not to hear, although it so happened that for once she had a good idea of what the picture was all about.

In between nibbling her breakfast that morning she had stared at it for a long time, trying to think what it reminded her of. Then it came to her. Once upon a time, a very, very long 'once upon a time' ago, she had been taken to stay with another guinea-pig. His name was

Boris, and he lived near the sea. The thing she remembered most about it was not so much Boris himself, but the smell of the sea air. She had never come across anything quite like it either before or since. Boris told her it was called ozone, although it seemed a funny name for something that smelt so clean and nice.

She sniffed the picture and decided the ozone must have been blown away. That often happened to smells. It was another thing she remembered about her visit—most of the time there had been a wind blowing.

'Wheeeee! You're quite right,' she squeaked. 'If you like, I'll tell you a seaside story, all about the time when there was a great big wind that was so strong it nearly blew all the

ozone away. Luckily there were some guinea-pigs around at the time and they tied themselves together and got in the way, otherwise goodness knows what would have happened. The world might have come to an end.'

Noel gave a snort. 'I don't want to hear any seaside stories,' he said gloomily. 'That's where everyone's going tomorrow. Everyone, that is, except us. They're going for two weeks.'

'Two wheeeeks!' Olga stopped dead in her tracks, a blade of grass half in and half out of her mouth. 'The Sawdust family are going to the seaside for two "wheeeks" and they're not taking me with them?' she repeated.

'*Us*,' said Noel. 'Not just *you*. They're not taking any of us. I heard them talking about it this morning. It's somewhere called "abroad" and if we go too we won't be allowed back in the country.'

Noel kept his ear to the ground and was usually the first to know what was going on—especially if it affected him in any way.

'Not allowed back in the country?' squeaked Olga in alarm, as the words sank in. 'Wheeeee !'

'Wheeee's right,' said Noel. 'Mind you, in your case I could understand it. I'm surprised they let you through in the first place. Graham and Fangio will be all right. They've got somebody coming in every day to feed them. I suppose I shall be going to the Bahamas as usual,' he added carelessly.

'The Bahamas?' repeated Olga. She felt a pang of jealousy. 'Where's that? Is it very far away?'

'It's just up the road,' said Noel. 'It's a place called "The Cattery". It's very popular—Mrs Sawdust says you have to book up months ahead. I usually meet up with a few old friends. Other cats who stay there every year.'

Olga quickly went off the idea. The thought of spending the time with a lot of cats wasn't her idea of fun, and she folded the blade of grass carefully in two so that she could eat twice as much at one go, in case the worst happened.

'Well, I hope they've booked up something nice for me wherever it is,' she said when she had finished.

'You're going to somewhere called Yuno Ware,' said Noel. 'I think it must be in China.'

'China!' squeaked Olga.

'Well, wherever it is, it's a long way away,' said Noel. 'Mr Sawdust had his maps out last night. It's on the other side of a river and I think it must be in China because I heard him say they could get a Chinese takeaway on the way back.'

'A Chinese takeaway!' wailed Olga. She still had vivid memories of a Chinese takeaway Mr Sawdust had brought home once before. He had offered her a bit to try and she hadn't liked it at all.

'But I don't like takeaways,' she said. 'Especially Chinese ones.'

'Well, you'll have to get used it,' said Noel. 'That's all they eat there.'

'But I want to know . . .' wailed Olga, as she felt her whole world begin to collapse about her.

'You'll see,' said Noel. 'Just you wait. You'll see.'

As things turned out, he was right. Olga certainly did see for herself, and she didn't have long to wait either. Noel had hardly left the room when Mrs Sawdust came in carrying a small plastic box lined with hay. The lid was open, and Olga's heart sank, for it usually meant she was being taken somewhere.

At least going to China would be different, but she didn't know what to expect, and Noel had been no help at all. She strongly suspected he didn't really know what he was talking about, and she spent most of the journey buried in the hay wondering what was going to happen to her next.

Luckily Mrs Sawdust had thought to put some food in too, so the journey passed quickly enough. And then . . . the car came to a stop and a moment later, after a bit of jiggling about, Olga heard a strange voice.

'Say hullo to Mr Gee,' said Mrs Sawdust.

Olga did her best, but before she had time to

utter a single squeak, she felt herself being picked up and wrapped in a towel until only the ends of her paws stuck out. Then, to her horror, without so much as a 'by your leave' she felt her toenails being cut.

'It doesn't do to let them get too long,' said the voice. 'Otherwise they start to curl back on themselves.'

Olga was most offended, although at least whoever it was seemed to know what he was doing, which was more than could be said for some people she knew. *Some* people she knew said silly things like, 'This is going to hurt me more than it hurts you!' when she *knew* it was the other way round.

It was simply a case of snip, snip, snip, snip, snip . . . until all fourteen of her nails had been trimmed. She hardly felt a thing and afterwards she had to admit they felt much better for it.

But no sooner had Olga recovered from her first indignity than she felt something very cold being pressed against her stomach, high up just under her chin.

'Nothing wrong with her heart,' said the voice after a moment or two. 'Strong as an ox. Beating nineteen to the dozen at the moment, but it'll soon settle down.'

Next, Olga felt a gentle but firm pressure from a finger and thumb on either side of her face and when she went to close her mouth she found she couldn't.

'Her teeth are fine, too,' was the verdict. 'Good for a few more years of eating yet.'

Well! thought Olga. I'm glad of that!

She felt very relieved, and her spirits rose even further when she was given a dandelion leaf. What a nice man, she thought. I think I shall enjoy being in China after all.

It was only then that she realized for the first time she wasn't alone. The room she was in was full of cages, and from each of them a pair of eyes was watching her every movement. Everywhere she looked there were eyes. She didn't recognize any of the occupants, but some had long fur and some had short; there were black ones, brown ones, grey ones, white ones,

and others yet again that were a mixture of all four.

Olga was so surprised she only listened with half an ear as Mr Gee introduced Mrs Sawdust to the other animals, and because of that she missed the very beginning.

'I call them my liquorice all-sorts,' he said. 'I've hardly got two pigs that look alike at the moment.

'The first one is an Agouti. They come in all sorts of different colours. Golden, silver, chocolate, cream . . . Unfortunately this one has a white patch on her back, so she won't win any prizes.

'The one with the very long flowing hair is Fred. He's supposed to be what's known as a Coronet but he's a bit of a mixture, so I'm afraid I can't put him in a show either.

'The other one with long hair—the one who looks like Dougal in *The Magic Roundabout*—he's a Peruvian. His hair is so long he has a job seeing out sometimes.

'And that one—Jilly, is a Golden Sheltie. She can't sit still for a minute.'

Well, thought Olga as the voice droned on, I've never seen such a funny looking lot of creatures in the whole of my life. It's no wonder the Sawdust family prefer guinea-pigs.

Her mind was in such a whirl it was a moment or two before she realized Mrs Sawdust was talking to her.

'Take care, Olga,' she said. 'See you in two weeks!'

'Two wheeeeks!' wailed Olga. The reason

why she was there suddenly came back to her. 'Two whole wheeeeeeeeks!'

'Oh dear,' murmured Mrs Sawdust. 'I almost wish we weren't going away.'

'Don't worry,' said Mr Gee. 'She'll soon settle down.'

And he was right. As the voices died away Olga picked up the dandelion leaf and carried on from where she had left off. Almost at once she felt better. There was nothing like a good dandelion leaf in times of trouble.

While she was nibbling she thought things through. Two weeks was only half as long as it had taken for Christmas to come round, and she had managed that. In any case, if the Sawdust family were going on holiday she was better off where she was. She had no wish to look after herself, thank you very much, and with Noel in the Bahamas there would be no one else to tell her stories to.

Olga decided that while she was there she might try some of them out on the other animals. After all, they couldn't help what they looked like, and just because they were Chinese there was no reason why they shouldn't enjoy them. With that in mind, she settled down to make the most of her stay.

'Now,' she called. 'First of all, I want to say how lucky you all are that I'm here.'

By the time Olga returned home, her new friends were feeling quite worn out. She'd had a very nice time with Mr Gee, but it was good to be back, even though she hardly recognized the Sawdust family, for they had all gone a funny shade of brown.

Although she wouldn't have admitted it out loud, it was even nice to see Noel again and to hear how he had got on in the Bahamas.

'It was all right,' he said, as he busied himself checking up on smells around the house. 'But there's no place like home. How was China?'

'China was lovely,' said Olga. 'And I didn't have to eat a single takeaway.'

'How about the other guinea-pigs?' asked Noel.

'Guinea-pigs?' repeated Olga. 'What guinea-pigs? They don't have them in China. I think I must have been the first one they had ever seen. That's why they made so much fuss of me. They even had a Mr Gee who cut my toenails for me. I don't suppose there are many guinea-pigs who've had their toenails cut by a Chinaman.'

'No guinea-pigs?' said Noel. 'That's not what I heard. I heard there was a whole room full of them. I'm glad I wasn't there. Did they keep you awake at night with all their squeaking?'

Olga stopped eating and stared at him, wondering for a moment if she had heard right. It wasn't possible. It simply wasn't possible. She took a quick look at her reflection in the water bowl, just to make sure and heaved a sigh of relief.

Noel was talking nonsense as usual. They had been nothing like her.

'Luckily, Mr Gee knows everything there is to know about guinea-pigs,' she said. 'And he's very nice, too. In fact, he's such a nice person I think he must have been a guinea-pig himself once upon a time.'

'Oh dear, oh dear,' said Noel, to the world in general. 'You can tell she's back!'

He was about to say a lot more, but when he turned round Olga had disappeared into her box.

He stared at the spot where she had been. What was it Mr Sawdust was always saying about people never seeing themselves as others saw them?

If it was true of people then, if Olga was anything to go by, it must be doubly true of guinea-pigs. Which didn't surprise him at all!

8
Olga's Choice

After the holiday things soon returned to normal. The Sawdust family lost their funny brown colour and in no time at all it felt as though they had never been away.

Fangio and Graham were happiest of all to see everyone back. According to Fangio, several times his supper had been put out earlier than usual and he had turned up only to find someone or some *thing*—probably a cat— had got there before him and eaten it all.

Graham had an even worse tale to tell. For the first few days the person looking after him had left his breakfast in front of a garden ornament by mistake and by the time he got there the birds had flown off with it; either that or squirrels. It was only when he got up very early one morning and sat down next to the ornament that the man realized what he had done.

In the meantime he'd had to make do with slugs and other odds and ends he managed to find in the garden, which wasn't easy in the summer when everything was dried up.

'Can you believe it?' he kept saying. 'Fancy mistaking a lump of old concrete for a tortoise!'

Olga could believe it. For one thing it wasn't just any lump of old concrete; it was shaped like a tortoise. It even had the same shell-like pattern of lines across its back. In fact, from a distance she had often made the same mistake herself. She didn't like to say so, but in many ways she preferred concrete. At least it didn't keep on grumbling like certain tortoises she could mention.

Then, the first Saturday morning after her return, Olga was having a go at her oats when Mrs Sawdust arrived back home laden with rather more carrier bags than usual.

'There are days,' she said, unloading them on to the dining-room table, 'when shopping for Olga is worse than shopping for a family of ten. The beans have to come from one shop, the lettuce from another, and neither of them have the kind of beetroot she likes—I have to go to a third shop for that. As for the carrots—I go somewhere else again for those, so I usually end up making a special journey. If I go in there after I've bought all the other vegetables they give me a funny look. I can't really explain they're for a guinea-pig who won't eat all the rest of the things they sell.'

'I don't see why you need to,' said Mr Sawdust. 'It's none of their business.'

'In that case, you can go next time,' replied Mrs Sawdust.

'Then there's her hay—she prefers it farm-fresh from your brother-in-law in Wales. Oats come from the pet shop, which is in quite the opposite direction to the rest of the shops. I tell you, it's very complicated—especially when some of them change their suppliers and I have to start all over again. It really needs a computer to keep track of it all.'

'Perhaps I could make you a chart to hang on the kitchen wall,' said Karen Sawdust. 'You could have different coloured flags showing where you go for everything—pink for the carrots, red for the beetroot, green for beans . . .'

'She can't be really hungry, that's all I can say,' broke in Mr Sawdust. 'If she was really hungry it wouldn't matter what things taste like or where they come from.'

'I don't know so much,' said Mrs Sawdust. 'You try forcing something down a guinea-pig's throat when it doesn't want it. It's worse than giving roast beef to a vegetarian. And in Olga's case you're liable to end up getting a good nip for your pains.'

'She doesn't even have to taste it,' agreed Karen Sawdust. 'She can smell something that isn't nice a mile away. If you ask me it has to do with all the chemicals they use these days. You never know what they spray on things to make them grow.'

'I suppose,' said Mr Sawdust thoughtfully, 'that's where the expression "being a guinea-pig" comes from. I mean they talk about people being "guinea-pigs" when they try things out to see whether or not they work.'

'That's a bit of a mystery, too,' said Karen. 'They're not really pigs—they're rodents. And they don't come from Guinea either, they're from South America. The Aztecs in Peru are believed to have originally discovered them. We've been learning all about it at school.'

Olga gave a squeak of excitement as she listened to the conversation with half an ear. She couldn't help herself.

'It ought to be possible to harness them in some way . . .' mused Mr Sawdust.

'You mean she could be a food taster like

kings and queens used to have in the old days?'
broke in Karen.

'I don't see why not. Even if the queen
doesn't want to make use of her, I imagine a lot
of firms would be only too pleased to have that
kind of information. They might pay a lot of
money to have their carrots tested before they
send them out. I could try asking one or two to
see what they say.'

'You're not thinking of sending Olga out to
work, I hope?' asked Mrs Sawdust.

'It's only a thought,' said Mr Sawdust. 'But it
does seem a pity to let a talent like that go to
waste. She might become famous.'

'They could put little stick-on labels on
everything,' said Karen Sawdust. 'OLGA'S
CHOICE, or something like that . . .'

As the voices died away Olga sat staring into
space. She could understand about labelling the
best vegetables OLGA'S CHOICE; that sounded
very sensible. Deciding which ones to label
would be no trouble at all. In fact, she wondered
why nobody had thought of doing it before.

But as for going out to work and being paid for eating carrots, that was quite beyond her understanding. Then there was the business about being a rodent. It was the first she had heard of it and she couldn't wait to tell Noel. He was always making rude remarks about the fact that she was a pig.

'You'll be pleased to know I'm not a pig at all,' she called a little later on, when he was passing by on his way out to the garden. 'I'm a rodent and I was found by an Aztec in Peru. I expect he was tired of having a cat for company and wanted something more interesting.'

Noel paused and stared at her. It wasn't often he was at a loss for a reply. 'Oh, dear,' he said at last. 'A rodent. That's not very good news. I'm sorry to hear that. I'm glad I'm not one. It's the same as being a rat; people are always trying to catch you. They have things called "rat traps". There's a great big spring inside with a lump of cheese on one end ready to catch the first one that goes past. As soon as it takes a nibble the spring comes down and . . .'

Here Noel made such a blood-curdling caterwaul he even made himself jump.

Olga quickly decided she might stay as a pig after all.

'Quite right,' said Noel, after he had recovered. 'Rodents have tails and you haven't got one. Besides, you don't like cheese and your nose is much too big to go inside a trap.'

'Anyway,' said Olga, 'I expect I shall be going out to work very soon, so you won't be seeing much of me.'

'I can't wait,' said Noel. And he arched his back and went on his way.

Olga gave a sigh. She went back to sorting out the oats in her bowl and very soon the whole thing might never have happened.

Then, one afternoon several weeks later, she was woken from her afternoon nap by a ring at the front door bell. It was followed by the sound of a strange voice.

'We do, of course, have our own panel of fully qualified tasters . . .' said the voice as it drew nearer. 'However, following your letter, I have been instructed to look into the matter . . .'

Before Olga had a chance to hide, Mrs Sawdust reached inside her house and picked her up. The next moment she felt herself in someone else's hand; a strange hand.

As far as Olga was concerned there were good hands and there were bad hands. There were people who knew at once how to hold a guinea-pig, and there were those who had no idea; they either squeezed so hard, making it hard to breathe, or they were so loose she had to cling on for dear life. The new hand was much too loose for her liking.

'I've brought along a selection of carrots . . . To make the test fair and above board, I really think she ought to be blindfolded . . .'

'Have you ever tried blindfolding a guinea-pig?' broke in Mr Sawdust nervously.

'Some people like living dangerously,' murmured Karen. 'Perhaps I could try holding something in front of her eyes?' she added.

Olga looked up and was just in time to catch a glimpse of the newcomer before the top half of him disappeared behind a piece of cardboard. She didn't much like the look of what she did see, for his face was covered in whiskers—just like a bird's nest.

She turned her attention to a row of carrots being held out for her inspection. It didn't need one sniff, let alone two, for her to know she didn't like any of them.

She felt very put out by the whole thing and she had certainly taken an instant dislike to the visitor, especially when he became impatient and began pushing the carrots against her nose.

Seeing that something was expected of her she sank her teeth into the nearest thing she could find. It was softer than she expected— more like a piece of beetroot than a carrot— and her teeth went through it and out the other side like a knife through butter.

For a split second there was silence, then a loud cry rent the air and the hand she had taken such a dislike to disappeared.

'Wheeeeeeeeeeeee!' Olga added her own

cry of alarm as she felt herself flying through the air. Then everything went black.

'Oh dear,' said Mrs Sawdust, as she closed the front door on their visitor, 'it's all my fault. I did say I needed a computer to keep track of all Olga's likes and dislikes. I never dreamed he would turn out to be from the very people whose carrots she never touches. No wonder she bit him when he tried to force one down her.'

'So much for dreams of fame and fortune,'

sighed Mr Sawdust. 'I don't think he'll be coming back in a hurry.'

'By the sound of it he won't be going anywhere in a hurry,' said Mrs Sawdust, as they made their way back into the dining-room.

'The thing is,' said Karen, pointing to a small figure lying in the hay, 'what are we going to do about Olga? She hasn't moved since I put her down and she doesn't even purr when I stroke her.'

9

Olga Turns the Corner

'I should never have given her to that wretched man to hold,' said Mrs Sawdust, as she joined Karen on the floor by Olga's house. 'He had no idea how to go about it. The trouble is it all happened so quickly.'

'It's a bit like the time she hurt herself when the kitchen caught fire,' said Mr Sawdust. 'She landed on the concrete. Remember?'

Mrs Sawdust gave a shudder. 'Don't remind me. I'd better ring Mr Gee. He'll know what to do.'

Normally Olga would have pricked up her ears at the news that she was going to visit China again, but she was still in a daze. When the man let go of her she had taken a flying leap into space, not knowing or even caring where she was going to land. Luckily the Sawdust family's room had wall to wall carpeting and that had helped cushion her fall, but even so it felt as though all the breath had been knocked out of her. As for her bones; she was sure all the bones in her body had got tangled up with each other and ended up in the wrong place.

While everyone was rushing around making phone calls and getting ready for the journey, Noel, who had been watching events from a safe distance, came across the room to take a closer look.

'It wouldn't happen to a cat,' he said, airing his knowledge. 'Cats can land anywhere. Besides, we've got nine lives. I heard someone say that on the television the other day.'

'That's only because cats are greedy,' groaned Olga, feeling she had to say something.

Noel ignored the remark. 'I expect if anything happens to you, Mr Sawdust will buy a flag and fly it at half mast. That's something else I saw happen on television. They might even show your funeral on the news. I'll make sure I watch it.'

'Thank you very much,' said Olga. She'd often thought Noel spent too much time watching the screen. Now she was sure of it.

'I was only trying to cheer you up,' said Noel. 'If you like, I could lick you better. That's another thing cats are good at.'

'No thank you,' said Olga hastily. She gave a shudder. Noel had a habit of sniffing around places she wouldn't dream of going anywhere near.

'Well, don't say I didn't ask,' replied Noel. 'But I'll tell you something. A cat will lick someone else better, but you won't catch a human being licking a cat in a hurry—or a guinea-pig.' And he disappeared in a huff just as the others started to return.

Mrs Sawdust brought Olga's carrying box, lined with the softest hay she could find, leaving Karen to follow on with a supply of freshly picked dandelion leaves from the garden and a handful of grass for the journey.

Shortly afterwards they set off. Mr Sawdust drove as carefully as he could, especially when they went round corners or down any roads that had humps.

'Fancy calling them traffic *calmers*!' he said more than once. 'I'd feel calmer if we could get Olga to you-know-where a bit quicker.'

China seemed even further away than Olga remembered it, and there were times when she thought they would never reach it. But at least the hay stopped her rolling about in her box, and Karen Sawdust kept the lid open so that she could reach inside and stroke her and help keep her upright.

'Well, now,' said a familiar voice when they arrived. 'What have you been up to, my girl?'

I haven't been *up* to anything, thought Olga, as gentle hands reached in and picked her up. That's just the trouble. I've been *down*.

A towel had been made ready, all bunched up at one end to support her back, and she lay where she had been put to await the worst, for she was still feeling much too weak to do anything except let things happen.

There wasn't any question of having her toenails cut this time. There were more

important matters to take care of. She could hear Mr Gee's voice droning on as he ran his hands over her; then, again very gently, began pressing things against her body.

'Her heart's nice and strong . . . Nothing wrong there. Lungs are OK . . . She's had a nasty shock . . . there's no doubt about that . . . not as light on her feet as she was . . . probably landed awkwardly . . . I expect it's her W-E-I-G-H-T.'

'W-E-I-G-H-T?' repeated Karen Sawdust. 'You mean wei—'

'Ssh,' said everyone else.

Olga didn't like it when the Sawdust people did what they called 'spell things out'. Noel always said it meant they were trying to keep quiet about something—like when it was time for him to visit the vet for his once-a-year 'jabs' and they knew he might try and hide.

'The trouble is,' said Mr Gee, 'you can never tell with guinea-pigs. Sometimes they just give up for no obvious reason. They seem to lose the will to live.'

Olga wondered what on earth he was talking about, but his next words cheered her up.

'She'll have to go into intensive care for a while. I won't keep her here. She'll be much better off in her own home . . .'

She tried giving a squeak to let everyone know how pleased she was, but nothing happened, so she carried on listening instead.

'She'll need plenty of green stuff so that she gets her vitamin C; grass . . . she might be off carrots for the time being, but cauliflower leaves are very nutritious. Not too much spinach . . . that might affect her digestive system . . . Grind up her oats and mix it in with celery juice. I expect she'll be a bit dehydrated and it'll stop it sticking to the roof of her mouth. Try varying it with some carrot juice one day and beetroot juice the next . . . I suggest you use a syringe to feed it to her— she probably won't be able to do it herself for a while. Then if she begins to show signs of getting better you can try her on solids again . . .'

'What do you think her chances are?' asked Mr Sawdust.

'Listen to the others,' said Mr Gee.

Olga tried pricking up her ears, but she couldn't hear a thing. All the other guinea-pigs—if that's what they really were—had gone quiet.

'That says it all,' said Mr Gee. 'But still waters run deep. There's no knowing with that pig. The next forty-eight hours should see her through the worst. After that . . .' He broke off and didn't finish what he'd been about to say.

If anything, the journey back took even longer than it had going. Mr Sawdust seemed to be driving even more slowly than usual and nobody said anything.

When they got indoors Karen Sawdust lifted Olga out of her travelling box and placed her on the floor just outside her house. She did her best to lift herself up, but when she went to move her legs, try as she might, nothing happened.

'Oh, Olga,' said Karen, as she gave her a helping hand. 'You mustn't give up. You simply mustn't. I don't know what we would do without you.'

For the rest of that day everyone spoke in whispers. Noel wasn't allowed anywhere near, and all the while Olga slept in her hay, only opening her eyes from time to time when anyone came to see her.

That evening she had the first of her meals through a syringe. At first most of it squirted onto her fur and Karen Sawdust had to stand by with a wet flannel to wipe her chin, but Olga soon got the hang of it. She even began to enjoy the sensation, although there were moments when so much food went down her throat at one go it made her choke.

'It's all right for some,' said Noel, when he was allowed back in. 'I saw you through the window. Lying on your back with your legs in the air and your mouth wide open. You want to watch a fly doesn't go in, or a bee!'

Olga ignored the remark. 'I'm under intensive care,' she said. Although at the same time she resolved to keep her mouth tightly closed when she went to bed that night.

Mr Gee telephoned several times over the next few days to see how she was getting on and to offer advice.

'He thinks we might teach her to swim,' said Mrs Sawdust after one such call. 'Apparently he's got one pig with rheumatism and he does several lengths of the bath every morning. It does him the world of good.'

'Perhaps Olga could have some armbands,' suggested Karen Sawdust. 'Like the ones I had when I learnt.'

'Where would you put them?' Mrs Sawdust sounded doubtful. 'I mean . . .' She glanced down. 'I don't wish to be rude, but . . .'

Her voice trailed away as two large round eyes stared back. There was really no knowing just how much Olga did understand.

'On the other hand,' broke in Mr Sawdust, 'it might get rid of some of her F-A-T. I could fix a sling on the end of a stick to take her W-E-I-G-H-T.'

Olga gave a sigh. There they were, at it again —keeping things from her.

All the same, one way and another it stayed in her mind for the rest of the day. The idea of being lowered into a bath full of water didn't appeal to her at all and that evening, after the Sawdust family had finished their meal and were watching television, she decided to do something about it.

What was it Mr Gee had said? 'Still waters run deep,' was one thing. And 'There's no knowing with that pig,' was another. She would show them.

It was Mr Sawdust who noticed it first; a tug on the end of a trouser leg. At first he thought he was imagining it. Then it happened again.

'Olga!' he exclaimed as he looked down. 'How ever did you get there?'

Olga could have told him; she could have told him how she had pushed so hard on the floor of her box it felt at times as though her legs might fall off. And how worried she had been that if they did and they fell in the sawdust and got swept up she might never see them again.

Karen Sawdust picked her up and gave her a hug. 'It's a pity you can't write,' she said. 'If you kept a diary you could write down what a special day it is.'

But I did write something down once,

thought Olga. When I first came to stay with you. I wrote Olga da Polga in the sawdust. If I kept a diary I would write 'Today I went for a long walk.'

'This calls for a celebration,' said Mr Sawdust. He went to the refrigerator and took out a bottle, and when he opened it there was a loud pop and a lot of bubbles came gushing out.

'I've been saving this champagne for a special occasion,' he said, filling three glasses, 'and I can't think of anything more special than this.'

Olga was allowed a sniff; but she didn't think much of it. There was a funny fizzy noise coming from the glass and the bubbles tickled the end of her nose.

'Perhaps it's just as well,' said Mrs Sawdust. 'There's no knowing what would happen if she took to it.'

Shortly afterwards Mr Sawdust took the box the bottle had arrived in, and with a knife he cut down one side and opened the whole thing out so that it made a tunnel.

'There now,' he said, as he placed it on the floor outside her house, 'you have your own special entrance.'

'It makes it more of a *château* than a house,' said Karen. 'Especially with the word *champagne* written on the outside for everyone to see!'

'A *château*!' Olga gave a loud 'wheeeeeeeeee'
—the first she had made for days, as she went in one end of the tunnel and a little while later, to a round of applause, came out the other end.

Mr Sawdust took a picture and Mrs Sawdust gave her some banana to eat after her long journey. Then they all waited patiently while she turned round and slowly made her way back the way she had come.

'Wheeeeeeeee!' she called, as she finally poked her head out through the opening. 'Wheeeeee! Wheeeeeeeee! Wheeeeeeeeeeeee!'

'What on earth was all that about do you think?' asked Mrs Sawdust.

Olga could have told her. Except, of course,

she already had, so there was no point in doing it again.

It meant cats may have nine lives, but if you're a guinea-pig you have to think yourself lucky if you have two. And I'm going to make the most of my second one. I shall never, ever complain again—especially now I live in a *château*.

OTHER OLGA DA POLGA BOOKS

The Tales of Olga da Polga

ISBN 978-0-19-275495-0

From the very beginning there was not the slightest doubt that Olga da Polga was the sort of guinea-pig who would go places.

Olga da Polga is no ordinary guinea-pig. From the rosettes in her fur to her unusual name, there's something special about her . . . and Olga knows it!

Olga has a wild imagination, and from the minute she arrives at her new home, she begins entertaining all the other animals in the garden with her outrageous tales and stories – but she still has time to get up to all kinds of mischief and have lots of wonderful adventures too.

Olga Meets Her Match

Just in front of her there was an opening in the wall of the main building which she hadn't noticed before, and standing barely a whisker's length away in the darkness beyond was another guinea-pig . . . For a moment neither of them spoke, and then the other stirred.

'You must be Olga,' he said. 'I was told you were coming.'

Olga da Polga goes visiting and meets Boris, a Russian guinea-pig. Olga and Boris become firm friends and Olga is surprised to discover that Boris can tell even taller tales than she can! Soon the time comes for her to return to her own garden, but Olga doesn't mind, she can't wait to tell the other animals all about her trip and, of course, her new friend, and she even gives them all a demonstration of her Russian dancing skills . . .

Olga Carries On

ISBN 978-0-19-275493-6

'Wheeeeeeeeeee!' squeaked Olga.
'Ombomstiggywoggles and Wheeeeeee!
Wheeeeeeeeeeeee! Wheeeeeeeeeeeeeeeeeeee!'

What can it mean? Olga isn't telling, but Noel,
Fangio, and Graham are *very* impressed. So are
Fircone and Raisin.

Fircone and Raisin? Who are they? Well,
they're newcomers to the Sawdust family home
who arrive just in time to hear Olga's first
attempts at poetry. They aren't lucky enough to
come in time to see her amazing bravery on the
day the Sawdust family kitchen catches fire,
nor do they know about Boris's attempts to
liberate her, although perhaps that's just as
well, for as usual Boris seems to come out on
top.

Olga Takes Charge

ISBN 978-0-19-275492-9

Olga was in a jam. In fact, that day she had been in a number of different jams, each worse than the one before, until her mind was in such a whirl she didn't know which way to turn.

Olga is a very busy guinea-pig. She attempts to save the Sawdust family from the effects of a drought, she participates in a sponsored squeak, and she even takes up jogging. But somehow she always manages to find time to delight her friends with her tall tales and far-fetched stories.

Olga Follows Her Nose

ISBN 978-0-19-275490-5

*She happened to be passing the French
windows and as she glanced out she saw a
FACE looking straight at her. It was pressed
hard against a pane of glass—a cracked one
Mrs Sawdust was always talking about having
replaced—and it was watching her every
movement.
Worse still, as Olga slowly backed away it
began licking its lips.*

Lots of exciting things are happening in the
Sawdust household, and Olga da Polga is right
in the thick of it! First, there's the strange
jigsaw puzzle which looks good enough to eat,
and then there's a mysterious visitor in the
garden who thinks that Olga looks good enough
to eat! And as if that weren't enough, Olga and
her friends hear some shocking news that turns
a perfectly ordinary day into 'Black Friday' ...

Michael Bond was born in 1926 and grew up in Reading, England, along with a dog called Binkie and three guinea-pigs named Pip, Squeak, and Wilfred. He began writing in 1947 while serving with the army in Egypt. Short stories and radio plays followed, but it wasn't until 1958 that his first children's book, *A Bear Called Paddington,* was published. The phenomenally successful 'Paddington' books eventually led him to give up working as a BBC television cameraman in order to write full time. Inspired by his daughter Karen's guinea-pig, he embarked on the 'Olga da Polga' series. In 1997 he was awarded the OBE for his services to children's literature.